MULTUGGERAH AND THE SACRED MOUNTAIN

illustrated by
DEBRA O'HALLORAN

written by
FRANK UHR

Published by
Boolarong Press
38/1631 Wynnum Road
Tingalpa Qld 4173
Australia.
www.boolarongpress.com.au

First published 2019

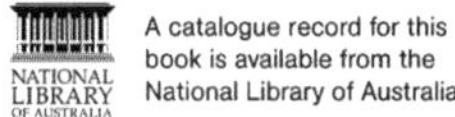

ISBN: 9781925877328 (paperback)

Cover artwork by Debra O'Halloran

Printed and bound by Watson Ferguson & Company, Tingalpa, Australia

Meet Multuggerah,
a First Nations Leader
from a long time ago ...

Multuggerah didn't like sheep much, nor did he like the men who put them on his country.

They spoilt the country, scared away the native foods, and fouled the water.

He worried for his people's future.

Multuggerah watched as the jackeroos* got their supplies by bullock drays.

* Jackeroos is a Yuggera word for ghost or stranger. Commonly used today for a young cattleman.

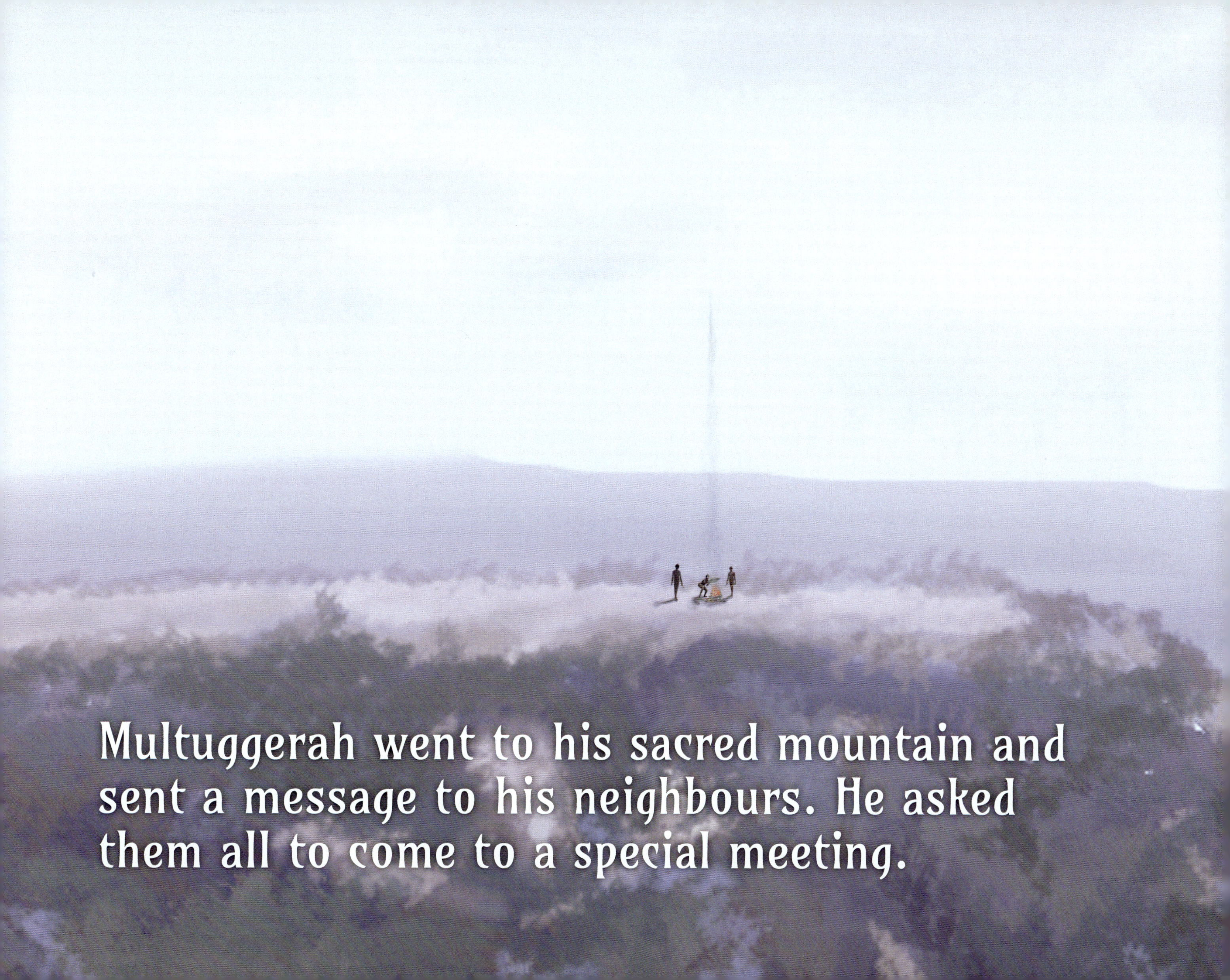

Multuggerah went to his sacred mountain and sent a message to his neighbours. He asked them all to come to a special meeting.

Six tribal leaders met on top of the sacred mountain. They all wanted to get the jackeroos to move away from their lands.

All the leaders voted to stop the drays on the mountain pass. This would stop supplies getting to the jackeroos and force them to move away to other lands.

A week later, Multuggerah and his allies prepared to ambush the men and their supply drays. They watched them come up the road.

The First Nations warriors threw their spears and shouted long and hard. The jackeroos leading the drays threw down their rifles and ran away.

The jackeroos ran as fast as they could, back down the road to where some more jackeroos were resting their horses.

Multuggerah led the warriors to the sacred mountain. They climbed to a ledge above the road and waited.

The jackeroos came galloping hard up the road to attack the First Nations warriors and save the supplies.

Seeing the First Nations warriors on the ledge, the jackeroos quickly dismounted and started climbing up the sacred mountain to attack them.

Multuggerah and his friends started rolling big rocks down the mountain at the jackeroos, who got back on their horses and rode away.

All the First Nations leaders were happy, and Multuggerah wished them all a safe journey home, knowing that they had won on the day.

Historical Note

Multuggerah, son of Moppy, (aka "Moppe" — "King of the Upper Brisbane") became leader of his clan in the Lockyer Valley on the death of his father at the end of 1842. He led the resistance in the Frontier Wars which included his famed ambush of jackeroos' drays on the road up the main range to the Darling Downs on September 12, 1843. He led warriors from at least seven allied peoples to a short-won victory at The Battle of One Tree Hill. He was killed three years later leading a raid on Rosewood Station in August 1846, but was mainly known for his ability to unite neighbouring clans into a guerrilla force of around 1200 warriors for their war against the white squatters.